For all my Nerdy Book Club friends from Nerd Camp, the Nerd Van, and the OG Crew—J.F.

For Josef Williams and the Rio De Janeiro class at Shirehampton Primary School —B.K.

STERLING CHILDREN'S BOOKS
New York

An Imprint of Sterling Publishing Co., Inc.
1166 Avenue of the Americas
New York, NY 10036

ISBN 978-1-4549-3427-1

Library of Congress Cataloging-in-Publication Data

Names: Funk, Josh, author. | Kearney, Brendan (Illustrator), illustrator.
Title: Lady Pancake & Sir French Toast : short & sweet / by Josh Funk ;
    illustrated by Brendan Kearney.
Description: New York : Sterling Children's Books, [2020] | Audience: Ages
    5 and up. | Audience: Grades K-1. | Summary: Fearing they are going
    stale, Lady Pancake and Sir French Toast visit Professor Biscotti, whose
    faulty gadget transforms them into toddlers, sending them on an
    adventure in the refrigerator.
Identifiers: LCCN 2019033156 | ISBN 9781454934271 (hardcover)
Subjects: CYAC: Stories in rhyme. | Pancakes, waffles, etc.—Fiction. |
    Food—Fiction. | Friendship—Fiction. | Refrigerators—Fiction.
Classification: LCC PZ8.3.F95926 Lak 2020 | DDC [E]—dc23
LC record available at https://lccn.loc.gov/2019033156

Distributed in Canada by Sterling Publishing Co., Inc.
c/o Canadian Manda Group, 664 Annette Street
Toronto, Ontario M6S 2C8, Canada
Distributed in the United Kingdom by GMC Distribution Services
Castle Place, 166 High Street, Lewes, East Sussex BN7 1XU, England
Distributed in Australia by NewSouth Books
University of New South Wales, Sydney, NSW 2052, Australia

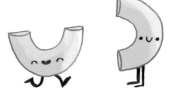

For information about custom editions, special sales, and premium and corporate purchases,
please contact Sterling Special Sales at 800-805-5489 or specialsales@sterlingpublishing.com.

Manufactured in China

Lot #:
2 4 6 8 10 9 7 5 3 1
06/20

sterlingpublishing.com

Lady Pancake & Sir French Toast

SHORT & Sweet

by JOSH FUNK   illustrated by BRENDAN KEARNEY

STERLING CHILDREN'S BOOKS
New York

Still in the fridge and behind the Swiss chard,
in their apartment on Crust Boulevard,
prepping a tea party, ready to host,
stood Lady Pancake beside Sir French Toast.

Just as they finished the boiling and baking,
Pancake said, "All of my muscles are aching."
"Also," said Toast, "my complexion is pale."
Pancake then screamed, "Are we both going stale?"

Baron von Waffle, their guest, said, "You're gruesome.
I've never seen such a hideous twosome."

The duo was shocked by their newly made friend.
Waffle went on, "I don't mean to offend.
In fact, it so happens there might be a cure.
Check out Professor Biscotti's brochure!"

Off to Professor Biscotti's they strode.
Down to her lab out by Artichoke Road.

"Greetings!" she said as she tightened a gear.
"Here for despoiling? Terrific! Sit here!"

Nervously, Pancake and Toast settled in.

"Explain what you did to them!" Waffle demanded.
Professor Biscotti said, "Hmm. I'll be candid.
I *over* de-spoiled them with my device.
I'm ever so sorry. I'll charge you half price."

Waffle stood fuming. His monocle shook.
"Charge us!" screamed Waffle. "They're children! Just look!"

"Eek!" shouted Pancake. "A waffle! I'm scared!"
"The monster will eat us! Let's run!" Toast declared.
"Eat you? I'm scary? No wait!" Waffle uttered.
"I thought we were friends. But—but—hey," Waffle stuttered.

Shrieking, the duo of pint-sized companions scampered and slid all the way to Bran Canyons.

and down through the Fjords of Farfalle, they splashed.

Out of the lab came a blubbering moan.
Baron von Waffle sat weeping alone.

"They were my friends,
but they ran off and fled.
Am I a monster?
'Cause that's what they said."

Professor Biscotti approached and began,
"My gadget—I'll fix it, but we need a plan."

"Phew! Are we safe now?" asked Toast at Pie Pier.
Pancake responded, "No waffles 'round here."
Then in the distance they spotted Limes Square.
Pancake asked, "Race ya?" And Toast said, "I'm there!"

Down to the city they skipped and they hopped.
until Pasta Playground, where both of them stopped.

Pancake played fetch with a little pet nugget
that scampered away when she offered to hug it.

Toast tried the see-saw,

the swings,

and the slide.

That's when he saw something better inside.

Waffle, still sour, knew just what to do.
"This is the bait that'll capture those two."

Biscotti kept working in her laboratories,

while Pancake and Toast sat enraptured by stories

until the two children inhaled something sweet,
and instantly both of them raced to the street.

They followed their noses past fjord, wall, and hill
and then kept on running and running until . . .

"The old syrup trick," Waffle said with a smirk.
"Professor, I've got 'em. So now will it work?"

She answered, "I hope so—or else this endeavor might cause your two friends to be children forever."

It whooshed and it whistled, except nothing sparked. "Something is missing," Biscotti remarked.

Waffle responded, "You've GOT to succeed."
"Okay . . ." said Biscotti. "But what does it need?"

"Yes!" said Biscotti. "Success! They've returned!"
Waffle, however, looked rather concerned.

Biscotti continued, "Cheer up! You look awful."
"They called me a monster. Remember?" said Waffle.

"So, *you* were the waffle," said Pancake, appalled.
"But *we* were the monsters," Sir French Toast recalled.

"Waffle, forgive us, dear friend," Pancake moaned.
"We're ever so sorry," Sir French Toast atoned.

Waffle stood silently, face filled with grief.
And then Waffle let out . . .

. . . a sigh of relief.
"I worried I'd lost my new friends," Waffle wailed.
"But everything's normal. You're back!" he exhaled.

"Waffle," said Pancake, "we'll always be chums."
"Exactly," said Toast, "till we wither to crumbs."

In the apartment, they finished their tea.
All of their aches and their mold ceased to be.

The trio felt splendid, in spearmint condition,
as friendship prevailed through their "small" expedition.